Tell Us A
Bedtime
Story

Read more books in this series:

My Family's Fantastic!

Will You Be My Friend?

TELL US A BEDTIME STORY
A PICTURE CORGI BOOK 978 0 552 57611 6
Published in Great Britain
by Picture Corgi, an imprint of Random House Children's Publishers UK
A Random House Group Company
This edition published 2012

3 5 7 9 10 8 6 4

Picture Corgi Books are published by Random House Children's Publishers UK,
61–63 Uxbridge Road, London W5 5SA
www.randomhousechildrens.co.uk
www.randomhouse.co.uk
Addresses for companies within The Random House Group Limited can be found at:
www.randomhouse.co.uk/offices.htm
THE RANDOM HOUSE GROUP Limited Reg. No. 954009
A CIP catalogue record for this book is available from the British Library.
Printed in China

Tell Us A Bedtime Story

Illustrated by Julia Seal

Picture Corgi

Once upon a bedtime . . .
Mum was out for dinner, Dad was reading his book,
and Lily and Tom were in a world of their own.

"I am the brave, handsome prince," said Tom. "And you," he snarled, glaring at Lily, "are the dreadful fire-breathing dragon."

"But I'm always the dragon," moaned Lily.

"Quiet, Dragon," shouted Tom. "Or I will have to fight you."

Suddenly there was a loud Grrrrrrrrrrrrr! from outside the door.
"An angry bear!" they both cried.

But it was only Dad.
"Now," said Dad. "I want less fighting, and more getting ready for bed."

"Only if you tell us a story," said Lily.
"And then tell us another one," said Tom.
"We'll see," said Dad. "But first it's bathtime."

So Lily and Tom jumped into the warm, bubbly bath that Dad had run.

"I am the fierce, adventurous pirate," said Lily. "And you are the silly, scaredy sea captain." And the pirate splashed the sea captain, sending water everywhere.

Arrrrrrroooooooooooooooo!

came a howl from outside the door.
"A big, bad wolf," Lily and Tom both wailed.

But it was only Dad.
"Now," said Dad, "I want a lot less splashing and a lot more washing. Do you want to hear that story?"

"Yes," said Lily and Tom quickly. "And then another one."

"Well chop-chop," said Dad.

So Lily and Tom washed their hair and brushed their teeth and got into their pyjamas.

"I am the strong and fearless knight," said Tom. "And you are the wicked witch," and they both whacked each other over the head with pillows.

But then there was a Rooooaaaaaaarrr! from outside the door.
"A horrible, hairy monster!" Lily and Tom both shrieked.

But it was only Dad.
"Now," said Dad, "I want far fewer pillows on heads and far more heads on pillows."

"Tell us a story, Dad," said Lily.
"Yes, and then another one," said Tom.

So Lily and Tom curled up together, and Dad got out their favourite storybook.
"Are you sitting comfortably?" asked Dad.
"Then I'll begin."

But as the story started it took on a life of its own . . .

Once upon a time there was a princess who wanted to get married and had to choose between a brave, handsome prince and a strong, fearless knight, so she asked a wicked witch to turn her into a dreadful fire-breathing dragon to see which of the two was the bravest. However, the witch fell in love with the prince and the knight and locked them in

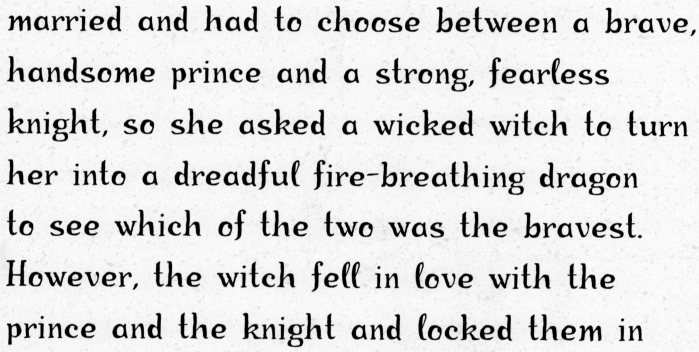

 a tower guarded by a horrible, hairy monster. Luckily a clever pirate who loved the princess stole the witch's spell book.

He turned the dragon back into a princess, the witch into an angry bear (who got into a fight with a big, bad wolf) and the monster into  a silly, scaredy sea captain who ran away. The princess could then choose whom she wanted to marry ~ the prince, the knight or the pirate. And of course she chose the pirate, as he was the bravest of all. And they all lived happily ever after.

The End

Dad was rather pleased with his story, but he didn't think he could manage another one.

Luckily, Lily and Tom had both fallen fast asleep.

Suddenly, Dad heard a TAP TAP TAP
from outside the door.
"A ghost?" he said to himself worriedly.

But it was only Mum!